KU-348-044

He sends his knights: One, Two and Three.
"Save the realm! But mainly me."

Knight One whispers to Knight Two,
"I've never seen a dragon. Have you?"

Knight Two says, "No. The king told me
they make the forest creatures flee."

Knight One says, "Well, the king confided

their spikes are thick and double-sided."

"Ha ha, ho ho," says small Knight Three.

"A bed of carrots won't hurt me."

Knight Two says, "Well, the king alleged

their teeth aren't used for fruit and veg!"

"Ha ha, ho ho," says small Knight Three.

"Sleepy beaks don't bother me."

Knight One says, "Well, the king declared

their necks are long, their nostrils flared."

"Ha ha, ho ho," says small Knight Three.

"A roosting post can't rattle me."

Knight Two says, "Well, the king forewarned

their tails stab the dark like thorns."

"Ha ha, ho ho," says small Knight Three.

"These snoring sentries don't scare me."

Knight One says, "Well, the king did stress

their flaming frying boiling scalding sizzling smelly breath!"

Knight Two says, "Dragons? No such thing.
Let's all go home and tell the king."

"Just as I thought," says small Knight Three.
"There's nothing here to frighten me."

"The dragon's just in the king's head.

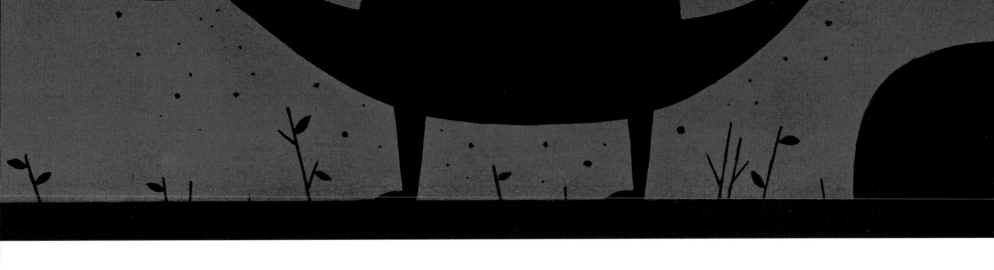

Good night, good knights, let's get to bed."

"There is no dragon taking wing.

The king is safe..."

"Long live the king!"

This edition first published in 2021 by Gecko Press
PO Box 9335, Wellington 6141, New Zealand
info@geckopress.com

English-language edition © Gecko Press Ltd 2021
Translation © James Brown 2021
Copyright text and illustrations © 2019 Leo Timmers
Originally published by Em. Querido's Uitgeverij, Amsterdam,
the Netherlands, under the title *Waar is de draak?*
Translation rights arranged by élami agency

All rights reserved. No part of this publication may be reproduced
or transmitted or utilized in any form, or by any means, electronic,
mechanical, photocopying or otherwise without the prior written
permission of the publisher.

Distributed in the United States and Canada by Lerner Publishing Group,
lernerbooks.com
Distributed in the United Kingdom by Bounce Sales and Marketing,
bouncemarketing.co.uk
Distributed in Australia and New Zealand by Walker Books Australia,
walkerbooks.com.au

Typesetting by Carolyn Lewis
Printed in China by Everbest Printing Co. Ltd, an accredited ISO 14001
& FSC-certified printer

ISBN hardback: 978-1-776573-11-0
ISBN paperback: 978-1-776573-12-7

For more curiously good books, visit geckopress.com